Five Without Honour Vol. 3

Copyright © 2024 Anxiety Press

All rights reserved. No part of this publication may be reproduced, distributed, or transmitted in any form or by any means, including photocopying, recording, or other electronic or mechanical methods, without the prior written permission of the publisher, except in the case of brief quotations embodied in critical reviews and certain other non--commercial uses permitted by copyright law.

Editorial Assistance – Elle Nash

ISBN: 9798326427939

Front cover image/interior design by:

ANXIETY DRIVEN GRAPHICS

Contents

7 *Reegan Brown -- Common*

23 *Wednesday Wilson -- The Art of Her Face*

26 *Chus Negro -- maze*

38 *Matthew Kinlin -- Sphere*

61 *Dakotah Weeks Murphree -- Exponential Growth*

Common

Reegan Brown

Honest tae fuck, a am sick tae the back teeth-- n a don't mean it in the generic "am fed up" way, a mean it physically makes me sick to the point ma back teeth fizzle n rot -- of seeing ma pals shrivel up n blister away in this desert waste -- land that naebdy seems able tae escape.

A stand behind this bar maist nights n watch them bouncing their sun--beaten, muck -- covered bodies intae the pub, greeting me wi' that tired and slightly amused "hiya hen," before they order a pint glass ae some amber liquid. As a pour, they hunch over the bar n glance about their local n try to look lit this isnae the only hing that's kept them gawn through the day. N ken the worst thing? The poor bastards are on fire n canny even smell smoke.

Ave noticed maist ae them give wee Ally's chair a cursory glance fae time tae time, thur's a wee joke about that chair, evdy is sayin it's cursed cause the past few occupants huv aw died within the past couple years or so. Ally was the most recent occupant of said chair, n the funny hing is he was the furst tae shrug aff the idea of a curse wae a laugh n a "wit a load a pish".

Ye kin see their shoulders drap as they trickle in one by one, congregating in pools of two or three before joining all together, like estuaries when they finally reach the ocean. N then a squad ae them head to the toilets, fags tucked behin their ears as they march dutifully in a line tae dae what they need tae dae. A forgot tae mention, this isnae me describing a weekend. A mean, it probably started aff as just a weekend hing but as these wee boys realised they were cursed wae the freedom tae day whitever they wanted, they stopped being held tae the cultural expectation that partying was limited tae the weekend.

Tae me, standing here cleanin' glasses, chatting tae the auld boys at the bar-- the right auld school wans that urnae shy to admit they're full -- blown alcoholics, there's something kinna sad aboot it. N a don't mean that judgemental or that, n a don't think for a second a can see anything these guys cannae. A think they all ken fine they're all just pretending life n drink n gear are aw still a gid time. Surely they *must* ken they're no actually enjoying themselves.

A always stand n yap tae Jim, wan ae the auld regulars at the bar. He's mibby 50 year auld but his face is lined beyond his years. He seems pure gruff n crabbit but he's actually no n we get a great laugh. A love Jim wae ma whole heart, a really dae, he pure looked after me when a wiz skint, fed me fae his ain kitchen when a ken fine he n his wife Jane were as skint as the rest ae us. Ye canny buy that kinna generosity n compassion. The man had three quid mare than fuck all n still managed to feed a daft wee lassie that hud just been kicked oot her maw n da's n wiz struggling tae keep herself fed. We spend hours shootin the shit n shakin wur heeds at the young wans that come in n hink they're it cause they've git a few quid in their pockets n some designer t-shirt slung across their back fae selling gear. Callum Mason's the worst wan by far, a pure big mouth n me n Jim canny stand him. Every time he opens his mouth me n Jim shoot each other a look that just says "fucks sake."

A never ken how to feel about the dealers in these groups, cause on the wan hand a feel like these cunts are killing their pals for a fuckin Gucci hat n some turkey teeth. Then on the other hand, wit chance hut they really hud? Wit options has society actually given them?

There's a funeral oan the day. Wee Davie Price, 28 years auld deid in the ground after he swallied fifteen Valium comin aff the gear n hung a rope roon his neck. Guess the comedoon wis that bad. Am workin the bar solemnly, ye don't crack jokes ir that on these occasions, a learnt that they hard way before when a made a wee jokey comment on the fact we'd hud the same five songs oan the jukebox for three hours straight. That went doon like a lead balloon let me tell you. This wans especially sad, it's always worse when it's a young wan. The boys all come in in their black suits n the lassies ur in their black dresses, mascara all smudged roon their eyes. They sit n talk n swallow spirits fae half -- glasses, gawn fur fags every time they finish their drinks.

A look round at evdy n think about how many times am gonny huv to work wan ae these. How many times am gonny have tae make awkward eye contact wae an empty bar stool that naebdy wants to sit in fur a few months because it reminds them ae somedy no here anymare. A mind the last time a hud tae dae this, when we lost wee Ally. The poor fucker lived upstairs fae the pub n was like an unofficial janitor -- emptied the bins fur me in exchange fur a pint. A went tae the funeral wae Jim, who wiz like a faither tae me. Singing the hymns wiz lit swallying golf balls, n the full village turnt up at the graveside, lined up ootside the cemetery. We aw kent it was the drink that killed Ally, his life hud went tae shit before he ended up huvin to stay above the pub. But as a watched his coffin getting lowered intae the soakin, freezing ground, ave never felt mare lit a murderer in ma life. His death paid ma wages. A traded a bit ae his life so that a didn't need to go ootside wae the bins.

This funeral's different though. Cause these boys huvny really been here before. They've went to wan ae these before, hung their heeds in respect for wan ae the auld boys but they've never lost wan ae their ane. The heavy atmosphere becomes charged wae a kind ae desperation and -- sure as fate -- they're aw away tae the toilets thegither again. A kin see the men's toilets in ma minds eye, a holy communion wae Callum Mason leading the service, placing the blood and body of Christ up his pal's noses and crossing himself wae their score notes. *"Save my soul father, save me from sobriety and the shit-- stained reality of this absolute cesspit we occupy."*

A kin see the lassies getting' riled up. Wee Davie's burd, Erin, is getting mare n mare steamin n ye kin see her jaw start to clench n the nostrils flaring as the water starts to threaten her thickly mascaraed eyelashes. A feel bad, a really dae feel bad fur hur. Aw these lassies huv the same experience, they've grown up wae these boys, some huv fell in love wae thum, hud relationships n weans wae thum. N now they huv tae sit n watch them drap lit flies, sit silently and keep their mouths shut as the faithers of their weans abandon them every Friday night no tae come hame til Sunday, maybe even Monday mornings -- if they come hame at all. Erin musta sat n waited oan Davie fur days oan end, phoning n phoning n then been so relieved n ragin at the same time when he finally dragged hisself oot ae witever hoose they hud been sat in fur aw that time. N then the next day he actually abandoned her fur gid..

A wonder wit that hoose must be like fur hur. A don't actually ken if it's worse noo that he's deed than it wiz when he wiz alive, n a don't mean that he wiz a bad guy or that his death isny a shame but the guy wiz hardly there. He wiz always away oot dain something wae the boys, away fishing n takin gear, away tae the fitba n taking gear, away tae the races or the pub or anywhere else but in the hoose, n takin gear. So on wan hand, they musta hud some gid times, they hud weans n aw that, but how many could that a been?

She stawns up, wobbles a wee bit on her awkward black heels n walks right up tae the group ae boys. By the way she's marchin a hink she's gonny swing fur wan ae thum. A huv this image in ma heed of her walloping Callum Mason clean across the face but instead ae the raised voices n character assassination that am desperate fur, their voices n heeds ur lowered. Callum nods n a kin see a wee smirk dancin' oan the edges ae his lips as his hand reaches intae wan ae his poakets. A stawn n watch, feelin lit a wean watchin the discovery channel, helpless as the drunk, grief --stricken antelope walks right up tae the Gucci--attired lion and asks him tae please, slowly, painfully, and wae a great, sick pleasure, please, put hur neck intae his turkey -- teethed jaws and fucking choke the life oot her.

It's awrite but, she kin pay the fifty -- quid fur the pleasure "jist when ye've goat it, hen."

He pits oan this kinnae friendly, sympathetic nod that wid turn yer stomach, as if he's no just charged a perfectly healthy, albeit completely devastated wee lassie nearly a days wages fur hur euthanasia.

The Art of Her Face

Wednesday Wilson

I am a wolf in woman's clothing.

A generational hangover.

In my three-- piece suit of finest human skin,

I walk around like my grandmother.

Fictitious, I just wish that I could ditch this masquerade.

I don't like the small talk and I think I over paid.

I don't understand the game or why it's being played.

But who are you when the mask is your face?

A patch work doll of other people's hearts.

Antipathic narcissist, my con is an art.

And to live up to the artifice is getting so hard.

But she does it with grace, and you sure love to spectate.

I thought myself into an early grave.

I left behind my skins and all my names.

With no character to play, what is left?

Miss Doesn't Fit has danced herself to death.

From the dirt, I rise.

Electric veins, fire eyes.

As I pulled myself together, I shook the earth.

Kicking and screaming, a natural birth.

I am not made from ribs.

My monstrousness belongs to me.

The seed is mine. I want to live.

The woman who would not lie down, beneath.

Lilith, Mother of Freaks.

Mary's Monster, walking alone on bloodied feet.

My own salvation, the apple eats the snake.

Finally, after all this time, awake.

Still, I walk.

I face the empty theatre.

I rip open my mouth and talk.

I am my own creator.

maze

Chus Negro

It was a place for us and then it wasn't. or it had never been a place for us, and at one point we came to realize the way it was. or we were truthfully invaders of the place, perhaps an aggregate plague. we were dark maybe. and that was bad, because they wanted to be happy, so happy and happy and happy and happy.

sometimes, daddy took us to the cabin, after a roughly one-hour walk through that old, uneven, earthy path. once there, all three of us sitting in those rickety wooden chairs, around that stale oak table, he would raise his (full) glass of wine above his own head, shaking it as without any control, and would start talking supposedly smart nonsense, in order to impress us, to patronize us, to dominate us, compelling full power, but, we indomitable creatures, loaded with rage and fear, it wouldn't work, so both you and me would keep staring at him in silence, wide-eyed, with lumps in our throats, expecting nothing from him but only that he wouldn't explode or get too angry. even if he actually hated we doing that, we couldn't help it.

"A good woman is not easy to find" -he would tell you- Not easy!" So, make a good woman of yourself... make... the greatest! The best! There is nothing else for you to do in live than that... Nothing, nothing nothing!!! Then, you'll have everything within reach! Everything you need! Everything you want! Every door! You'll find every door open up to you, only if you strive for being a good woman!"

the basic words would trigger along those lines, but the speech itself could get perfectly circular and endless, until he himself got tired of lecturing us (you, us), or got angry for having been talking so much and we being there like that, staring in silence, still but terribly frightened, hating too. many times both things, gab and anger, would come together, merged sometimes, sometimes simply correlated, with clear precedence of one over another, but not always in the same order. either from talking to angry, on account of the prate itself, or the angry talking manner instead, threading the words out of rage, they would come, the fearsome pairing would come, language and rage.

on one occasion, you said you didn't want to be some good girl, nor anything near to that. you made the toll payment. you couldn't get out of your bed like in five days. one of those nights, within those five days, i reached out stealthy to check up on you, and no sooner you saw my little fuzzy eyes appearing behind the half-open door you called me a coward.

"Why!?" -I complained- "Why do you call me that?!"

but you only repeated the word: "Coward."

and then again and again: "Coward... Coward... Coward..."

then I kept complaining, in severe distress, going mad. but you said nothing more.

it was already engraved over the air anyway.

I know, I knew, why you called me a coward. I was a coward. everyone was a coward. but I was the only one on your side. your side of the bed. your side of the woods. sometimes we kept talking until it was near morning, and we dreamt of a better place, remote but real, where pain was paid in blood. sometimes I felt the need to bury you, to embrace them, but in the end, I always came to understand right away that they, by their side, wanted to bury me, so I quickly went back to the only spot I was able to hold. against.

in order to not being devoured by the wild beasts, you tried to be the wildest of them, the wildest one, the one and only. sometimes I see you running wild through lands covered by tones of snow, standing up to forge your way to a safer place. a safer place. not the place. sometimes I can feel a work you made, inside me, sometimes I don't know what I am going to do with that, something that saved me and now I have to bear with. true; whatever it is, that work made by you, that work made inside me, I am alive because of it. sometimes routine is kind of annoying. sometimes I reduce everything to the tiniest thing, a smell, a gust of wind, anything that is ugly but striking, an unexpected or unidentified word, and then, I can move forward. that's a work made by you too.

when we were so small and so fragile, I remember looking at the things we were surrounded by, and not understanding anything at all; even the same old green grass was a mystery to me, because everything was elusive, because I had been launched to a world I could never be able to comprehend, nor even in its more basic, its more trim, expressions. sometimes it got me amazed; sometimes, most of the time, it prevailed over me, it drowned me, with its predatory embrace.

I remember me getting out of bed. I was thirsty, so I walked to the kitchen for a glass of water. almost immediately, I felt in the air that something was operating in a different mood; the message carried by the particles usually floating on the atmosphere had been altered by way of brute force. as when we laughed at daddy (then, making the toll payment). I went upstairs. first, I came to your room, I gently opened the door, and I saw you curled up under the blankets; if they were white and clean I did not consider nor care at that moment. everything was broadly the same as always, the same as every other night I entered your room, but with a stained set anyway. then, I went to mum and dad's, and, almost immediately, I saw that streaming out of there, flowing out from underneath the door, thankfully hypnotizing, as if the liquid was bright live fire. I felt the urge to drink it, to get down onto hands and knees and lick it from the floor, but I hold myself back, completely back, downstairs, to my room, to my bed, where, then, I took rest.

sure, childhood was astounding and colourful as every childhood unavoidably is, and our ranges were primarily shades of grey. not grey for equilibrium nor for a kind of impossible mixture of bad and good, but for hiding the colours as a strategy, for having the hues, but not the paint. sometimes I sit down, on the old green grass, and I look to a dying skyline. secrets are killed by time, but their remnants stand mixed up with the sap of the earth. I was born on some ordinary day, coming to a world smudged with the birth of others; now I am still here, wondering, reflecting on language and anger, on power might authority / affection rejection cowardice / weakness fragility rage, and how some beautiful joyful lovely puddle could beamingly take a place where there was total despair, I get awed by the odd fact that I am still here, sat down, feeling the young and fresh green grass.

Sphere

Matthew Kinlin

Mackerel sky swam across the blank face of the police officer. His freshly shaved skin hid the despair blistering beneath. Over the course of the last four days, he had swallowed back mouthful after mouthful of his anger. It lived inside his chest now like a black orb. It acted with its own secret design. Staring through the reinforced window of the cell, he remembered how much he hated Glasgow: endless rows of slum tenements, the dark mauve walls that dragged down and devoured rainbowed arcs of light from above. Empty--faced phantoms stalked its streets. It was an uncertain and pale realm, riddled with capricious doubts. Czapski had arrived earlier that week, ejected abruptly from his bucolic English village life, into a train carriage and taxi, then on to police headquarters in Ibrox. Clouds rushed backwards across the flat land. He remembered a promise he once made to himself never to return to this place.

"And what time did you last see her in the apartment?" Czapski asked.

"Midnight! I've fucking told you! We were watching television and she went into the hallway."

"She went into the hallway."

Czapski repeated the sentence in the hope it would finally make sense to him.

✳✳✳

Neither of them wanted to lock eyes any further. Their exhaustion was mutual. The insipid stalemate of his questioning had been reduced to empty respiration, cold droplets of water on the surface of the two--way mirror. His breath had combined with Ricardo McIntyre's, the latest partner of his sister who had lived with her for the last eight months in Riddrie, a north--eastern district of Glasgow. The witness continued to speak. Czapski resented his powerlessness that Ricardo diligently explained back to him, again and again.

"It's been happening all across the city. You've read the news. They see it in the sky. A flying saucer above Glasgow. Then a day, a week, a month later," Ricardo clicked his fingers loudly, "Pop! They vanish."

Czapski couldn't listen to the insanity any longer. He considered asking the other officer to step inside, the one with the neck tattoo. Czapski instantly smelled the violence on him. Two years ago in Brixton, he watched three police officers break a suspect's arm. They marked it down as physical restraint. There were pressure points you learned to target: the brachial plexus, the hypoglossal nerve along the jawline. In fleeting moments he felt sick in his complicity with a bankrupt institution. Other times, he enjoyed enacting misery upon another body.

"She was taking T--P8s, you stupid fucking pig."

Czapski's forearms tightened. Knocking on the mirror, he signalled for someone else to take over. Ricardo was dragged away to a holding cell. Czapski sat for a further few minutes in the interview room. He drank the cold polystyrene cup of coffee, trying to regulate his breathing.

※※※

He would never have come if it had been anyone but his sister. *It's Maja*, said the voice on the phone. On the table of the interview room were hundreds of pencil drawings of intergalactic beings with sad opalescent eyes. Blue amphibians scribbled and soared above monolithic buildings, amphibians crawling across the concrete Gorbals. A mosaic of paper eventually formed, showing Glasgow covered in loops of orange radioactive, the red revenge of dwarf stars smeared across the northern hemisphere.

Once more he pressed the button of the recording machine to play the mp3 file uploaded from Ricardo's voicemail: *There's a spaceship above Glasgow. It's this incredible fountain of light and energy.*

Frustrated, he swept away the drawings then folded them into his backpack. The sun was setting as he headed back to the cheap Premier Inn hotel down the M8 motorway, the rain -- sodden Braehead shopping centre dissolving in the distance.

He tried not to think about it. His sister in the council flat in Riddrie, taking pill after pill. Over the course of an evening she flooded her body with azure sleep. The effects of T--P8 had been widely reported in both national and global news: similar to benzos in their downer effects, but with specific psychedelic phenomena. T--P8 had become infamous for its unique link with Glasgow. Users of T--P8 consistently reported seeing a spacecraft above the city. From the start of this year, the media tied a rise in civilian disappearances with T--P8 use. There had been eleven local disappearances in the last month alone. Czapski thought of his sister stood in a hallway of white Artex plaster. He had studied the crime scene images. The vacant lightbulb above. The photograph of her first communion nailed to the wall. Ricardo watching television in the next room as Maja began to see her arms glow. Slowly, the flesh became translucent.

✖✖✖

Weeks passed and eventually Czapski's wife stopped calling. The disappearance of his sister proved a helpful catalyst for their imminent divorce. In the soulless hotel room, he read thousands of online articles about alien abductions: sepia images of American Midwest farmers stood in fields of ruined wheat. They spoke about concentric shapes that communicated directly with the Andromeda Galaxy. He saw the naked body of Maja asleep inside a dark boat. Her breasts were covered in red burns. He remembered his sister as a teenager running through a city square in Kraków filled with greenfinches. He saw her levitating in a black chapel in the village. A plastic tube entered a hole in her neck.

Startled, he woke from the sweating nightmare. His phone was flashing loudly on the bedside table.

"Officer Czapski," said the voice, "This is the control room. I'm just letting you know that

CCTV has made a possible match with your sister down in HouseHillwood. She has been seen buying illicit substances with a young male on Peat Road. We thought we would inform you. Two patrol cars are trying to locate them."

XXX

His hands shook as he gathered his clothes off the floor and unlocked the hotel safe. Inside was a standard issue handgun. The air in the carpark danced ice --bright and painful along his fingertips as he struggled to start the car. The streets to the southwest of the town centre were filled with low, pebble -- dashed houses. A jagged shadow, preparing for work, froze inside an amber bathroom window like a winter phantasm.

It wasn't hard to reach them. Their Fiat Punto swerved all over the road. Suddenly, they changed direction and headed back to Govan on towards the city. Both cars sped forward and followed the river that fed on itself like a pewter snake. Large blocks of concrete hovered mid--air above unfinished building sites. Invisible men in orange hi--vis emerged from overnight portacabins in clouds of peppermint vape. An Ibrox plot of wasteland glistened with green and broken glass. The city expanded around them as Czapski accelerated through the insidious, sprawling web.

The police radio informed Czapski there were two patrol cars nearby but none could be seen. The suspects continued northeast. A church spire corkscrewed into morning air above the Necropolis, its hillside graves burnished ochre in the first shivers of dawn. Czapski could only make out the indigo shape of the driver. He expected them to turn for Riddrie towards his sister's flat, but the car headed north. They drifted softly from the motorway into labyrinthine suburbia.

Eventually, the Fiat stopped in front of an area of deserted land. Along its western perimeter stood the remains of an enormous derelict building that must once have been the main block in a housing scheme. Czapski quietly pulled in behind them and parked.

A girl leapt from the car. Her body was sharp and angular, hair flowing in blonde hurricanes. Another figure in a navy hooded jacket emerged and grabbed her by the wrist. 'Police!" shouted Czapski, yanking open his door, "Stop right there!"

The man dragged the girl towards the building through a large hole in the wire fence. Czapski reached for his gun. He could hear the girl laughing hysterically.

Czapski quickly crawled through after the pair. The doors of the high--rise had been completely destroyed. Its concrete walls inside were filled with bizarre symbols. He used the light on his iPhone. They looked like scientific equations: one described the gravitational pull of a black hole; another a S--type star.

There was a sudden bang. Spinning around, Czapski dropped the iPhone to the ground. He automatically reached for his gun. He walked from corridor to corridor as laughter and footsteps running up the stairs echoed from above.

"Come down!" he screamed, but there was no reply.

Czapski sprinted up the stairs after them. He turned a corner when a blinding and terrible blow hit the back of his head. Stunned, he fell to the ground. The impact was a wall of white shock. Dazed, he looked up to see the hooded figure holding a large iron bar. The girl was out of focus. He heard the bar fall loudly to the floor as the couple walked away into an adjacent room.

After a few moments, Czapski staggered back onto his feet. He placed his hand to the back of his head and touched a slipperiness of blood that streamed from his broken skull. His vision burned pink. His arms shook uncontrollably as he tried to hold the gun again.

In the next room, the girl was leaning across the far wall. Her stance was relaxed and playful. She was whistling. Through the pulsating blob of bright pain, he stumbled towards her.

"Maja?" Czapski called out, desperation rising in his voice.

Suddenly, the hooded figure walked towards him from a corner adjacent to the entrance of the room and pushed him back to the floor. The man kicked the gun from his hand. His mouth was moving. It was jarring for Czapski to realise that the stranger was talking in Polish.

"The god here is a jealous god," the hooded figure said, "It has bathed in the waters of these silver and miserable lakes. Its emaciated body emerged in zirconium from the shores of Loch Lomond."

Czapski's arms fell weakly to his sides. He watched the shadow of the girl sway across the wall as the stranger continued to speak.

"Do you remember Holy Saturday? You were supposed to go to Kraków with your mother but you both ran away, into the forest. You could see the moon even at midday, yes?" The figure began to laugh to himself. The strength completely drained from Czapski's body. "She had made love to every boy in the village by that point. And your poor mother, she lost her mind not long after. Maja loved to walk through those fields at nights. That day felt like night, didn't it? She was covered completely in violet and copper butterflies."

The figure came closer now. The head inside the hood looked like it had been grafted from many faces.

"Who...?" Czapski managed to stutter.

He watched as the girl revealed herself in the vague glow of the city. She looked nothing like his sister.

"Have you ever seen a UFO?" she whispered, raising her fingertip towards the concrete windowsill.

❌❌❌

Sadly, Czapski shook his head. And taking a small inhalation of breath, he looked up. The shape in the sky was a sphere. It reflected his own alabaster face as blood drained weakly from the scalp. It was his skull collapsing backwards through a Glaswegian walkway, canals of haemoglobin pooling around a concrete room where his sister ate and dreamed beneath envious wings erupting from unknowable bodies. The shape was a star that fed on human sleep. He let out a final whimper as the girl moved towards him and pushed the cold barrel of the gun deep inside his mouth. A faint crackle rose from the obliterated lungs. The sound of a skeleton betrayed by gravity.

Exponential Growth

Dakotah Weeks

You're going to change the world, he said.

Looking up at him looking down on me, this was a tempting thought. The pride and conviction it took for him to say this to me caught me off guard.

How would I change the world?

Or, why would he think that?

I looked into his eyes and believed.

※※※

My boyfriend Venmoed me $500 towards "living expenses." This was, in my mind, part of a tab I knew I would eventually pay off. In full.

After a long night of fucking and a long morning of playing house, I was exhausted.

The sun was setting earlier and earlier, and I was tired of hearing my roommate work from home through our shared wall.

I met Sylvia soon after she'd arrived in the city. Her face was fresh, like her attitude and her way of speaking.

She would take my notebook and compose whole poems in minutes. She would cut holes in the crotch of my tights and leave a note saying, "Be good."

We used to hide out from the mouse that lived in our kitchen in Sylvia's room. I was terrified, as was our cat. Sylvia and I fell asleep in her bed, our hair braided together.

Now that Sylvia had a serious job, it was I alone who cleaned our Brita filter and dutifully fed the pigeons in the park each morning. I spent my time burning out on the fire escape while Sylvia stayed on Zoom. I relaxed into the heat and allowed myself to be infinitely placated by my own idealism.

Maybe I was naive to want all the things I wanted, to want them all at once. But weren't the most seductive voices the ones promising our wildest desires?

I had drinks with my professor, the one writing the book about the history of the world through advertising. Obviously a genius. His head was incredibly large and his eyes were incredibly small.

I remembered the rumor I'd heard about him my junior year; that he had a threesome with two of his students, causing one to have a nervous breakdown and drop out weeks before presenting her dissertation.

When I went to order at the bar I'd been carded. I know he found this amusing, a chuckle with a squeeze of my arm.

The bartender said, "You're 24?"

I said, "How old are you?"

"24."

We locked eyes for a moment after that, then he went to work filling two cups on opposite sides of the bar.

The exchange reminded me of waitressing as a teenager; my coworker had a habit of saying, "Older than me! You're older than me!" when she checked IDs.

I knew this exchange was particularly off-putting because she looked so much older than she really was. The customers recoiled as if looking into a trick mirror. Could that be so?

"He likes them young," an onlooker said. This felt harmless to me as I did not feel young anymore. I was safe.

XXX

I dreamed in menus. Of all the things that I would cook, and you would eat. I dreamed of dressed tables, set with napkin rings.

I dreamed of ironed table cloths. I dreamed of birds, and stuffing them.

I dreamed of preheating. The flame of the gas burner.

I wanted to open all the drawers, to see the shine of the cutlery, the starch of the dish towels, the stature of the mixing bowl.

I prayed every day for complete surrender, and I found it at night, in my kitchen fantasies. Providing a warm meal for you.

XXX

It was Sylvia's birthday today. Her boyfriend bought her a black wallet costing $300. This was to replace the wallet from her last birthday which had gotten worn out. Tilting back my champagne flute, I looked through the glass at her incredibly beautiful friends. I wondered how Sylvia had privately sold me to them. What did I have to offer in a world of bankers, private equity protectors, influencers, and boutique graphic designers?

"This is my roommate… we live together."

Sylvia sat me next to a girl she'd met in an old coding class a couple years earlier. She was also unemployed, which made me feel like children at the adult's table.

I knew we wouldn't get along. Vivian was stunning, she considered herself a hacker and I'd read lines of 0,1,0,1 she'd written as poetry in a popular alt magazine earlier this year. She told me about her communal household and her pet snake. I thought I felt her foot on my leg under the table for a moment. I blinked and it was gone; was it ever there?

The conversation shifted, echoing outward from the center of the table so that even us at the end could absorb some of it. The girls were discussing an app. This app had just been given the highest recognition at Sylvia's company.

The app literally gives refugees cryptocurrency based on how much they are walking. Their steps mine the virtual coin.

"What are refugees going to do with Bitcoin?" I ask.

"So actually, it's Ethereum, and um, yeah I too had skepticism about the app but their presentation was so comprehensive and ultimately, I do think we lost out because while we focused soooooo much of our time on user interface I do think we, ultimately, forgot that as our company grows, it needs to really align itself with certain social causes, like, that is growth! That's how growth happens. Not to mention putting our technology in the hands of new users, expanding that database. So yeah, they just really did a great job matching our values with honestly, like, making the world a better place."

I nodded.

Was a company's growth the measure of its goodness?

Sylvia's boyfriend tallied up the bill. He put it all on his credit card. He wanted the points.

XXX

Being so far away from home, adrift in a sea of opportunities, I often thought of what would make my mother happy.

This was the measure of success I knew most intimately, the one I had been learning my entire life.

XXX

I did imagine it would be fun to sleep with Richard, but this was when I was a student, gorgeous and vapid. No perfume but my naiveté filled every room I deigned to walk into.

And I walked into every room open to me, promised something or nothing, it made no difference. I once let a boy into my apartment because he'd lent me his umbrella on a rainy day. Another time, I slept on the floor of a man's bedroom who owned no furniture. He had a huge penis.

Now that I was out of school, there was no shock and awe to the idea of seducing Richard, or rather, allowing him to seduce me. I convinced myself I was dressed unremarkably and modestly as I made my way towards his reading in NoHo.

I watched him move under the harsh lights, as the crowd grew quiet to listen. "In fantasy, we are our most real selves…"

And so he launched into it.

Richard's colleague Andrew was enthusiastic to meet me, with a firm handshake and eyes ablaze. He immediately started scanning the room when he learned I was a former, not current, student. Soon his body followed where his eyes had landed. I turned back as he shoved past me, squaring up next to two girls turning pink with laughter.

I walked swiftly toward the exit, moving like I was eager to see how many pieces of something I could leave in my wake.

✷✷✷

My boyfriend tells me he wants to give me everything.

He tells me there's nothing he has that I won't have.

He arrives late so there's only darkness.

He wants me to thank him.

He wants me to tell him he is good.

He will believe me when I tell him.

The room is so quiet only the fan's whirring.

There's nothing to see in this room but the two of us.

He promises me he'll always love me.

He knows this is a great gift.

✖✖✖

When a man grabs my ponytail on the subway ride home, it scares me how good it feels. I almost forget to react. I turn around and meet his eyes. He must be crazy. Now I could tell.

Bios

Dakotah Weeks Murphree is a writer and performer born and raised in Birmingham, Alabama. You can find her between Berlin, NYC, and Glasgow.

Reegan Brown is from the West Coast of Scotland. She completed her masters degree in English at Strathclyde and loves every kind of literature, from Euripides and Homer to Kerouac and Ginsberg. In her spare time she reads constantly and tries to spend as much time outside as the Scottish weather and her schedule will allow, which isn't as much as she'd like. She's spent a lot of time working in pubs and finds inspiration in the anecdotes of those who come in for a pint. Reegan thinks life is made up of these little funny stories and asides and loves to hear them. Her Instagram handle is: @is___this____it

Wednesday Wilson is a graduate of Dundee University with an Honours Degree in English and Creative Writing. She has performed spoken word poetry throughout Scotland and is currently writing her first novel.

Chus Negro was born in Toledo (Spain) in 1981 and raised in Pola de Siero (Asturies), he works professionally as a translator and proofreader, and is the author of two published books of poetry, *Historia del tiempo presente* (KRK, 2005) and *mientras*

dormíamos la gran siesta y *mientr▲s dormí▲mos l▲ gr▲n siest▲* (Trabe, 2017). he also has appeared in different anthologies and magazines.

Matthew Kinlin lives and writes in Glasgow. His published works include *Teenage Hallucination* (Orbis Tertius Press, 2021), *Curse Red, Curse Blue, Curse Green* (Sweat Drenched Press, 2021), *The Glass Abattoir* (D.F.L. Lit, 2023) and *Songs of Xanthina* (Broken Sleep Books, 2023).

RE-EDUCATION

ANXIETY PRESS

ES TD

20 20

COMMUNITY

CAMP

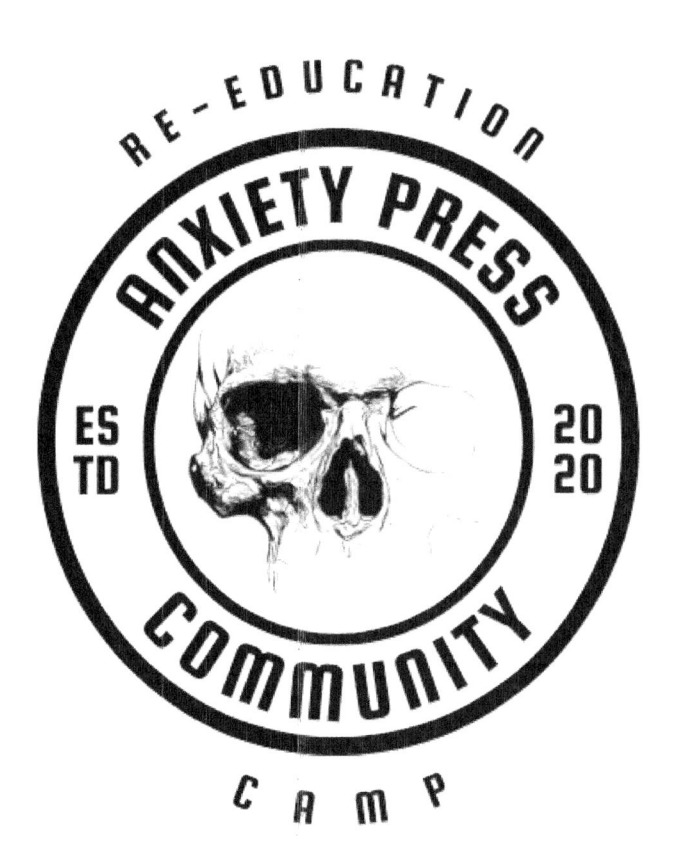

Printed in Great Britain
by Amazon